BLUE MAGIC

Books published by Red Fox in the Read Alone series

The Trouble with Herbert
Herbert Saves the Day
Stinky Cynthia
by Heather Eyles

Trouble Next Door
Philomena Hall and the Great Gerbil Caper
by Roy Apps

Henry's Most Unusual Birthday
by Elizabeth Hawkins

My Kid Sister
by E.W. Hildick

Cat's Witch
Cat's Witch and the Monster
Cat's Witch and the Wizard
by Kara May

I Want to be on TV
by Penny Speller

The Great Blackpool Sneezing Attack
by Barbara Mitchelhill

Stanley Makes it Big
by John Talbot

Blue Magic
Amos Shrike, the School Ghost
Snakes Alive!
Through the Witch's Window
by Hazel Townson

Lily and Lorna
The Salt and Pepper Boys
The Pop Concert
by Jean Wills

Rolf and Rosie
by Robert Swindells

Wilfred's Wolf
by Jenny Nimmo

Cabbages from Outer Space
by Lindsay Camp

BLUE MAGIC

Hazel Townson

Illustrated by Mary Rees

Greetings to St Philips!

Hazel Townson

5.2.96

RED FOX

A Red Fox Book
Published by Random House Children's Books
20 Vauxhall Bridge Road, London SW1V 2SA

A division of Random House UK Ltd

London Melbourne Sydney Auckland
Johannesburg and agencies throughout the world

First published by Andersen Press Limited 1992
Red Fox edition 1993

5 7 9 10 8 6

© Hazel Townson 1992
Illustrations © Mary Rees 1992

The rights of Hazel Townson and Mary Rees to be identified as the author
and illustrator of this work have been asserted by them in accordance with
the Copyright, Designs and Patents Act, 1988

This book is sold subject to the condition that it shall not, by way of trade
or otherwise, be lent, resold, hired out, or otherwise circulated without the
publisher's prior consent in any form of binding or cover other than that in
which it is published and without a similar condition including this condition
being imposed on the subsequent purchaser

Printed and bound in Great Britain by
Cox & Wyman Ltd, Reading, Berkshire

RANDOM HOUSE UK Limited Reg. No. 954009

Papers used by Random House UK Limited
are natural, recyclable products made from wood grown in
sustainable forests. The manufacturing processes conform to
the environmental regulations of the country of origin

ISBN 0 09 966870 X

Contents

For Margaret Craik

Your library is precious — Use it or lose it!

Chapter One
In which a Witch Comes to School

Wham!
Bella the Bully slammed her fist
into Skinny Lizzy's school-bag.

'Next time it'll be your face!'
yelled Bella, zooming off across
the playground.

Lizzy Lee mopped up the
squashed tomato inside her bag.
'One day,' she thought, 'I'm going
to get even with that girl.'
But when the odds are against
you, how do you get even
with somebody twice your size?

Just then, a funny old woman
leaned over the railings
and dropped something into the
playground.

Lizzy ran to pick it up,
and wow!
It turned out to be
*A Witch's Own Book of Magic
Spells!*

Lizzy called after the witch, but
she did not hear.
(Perhaps she should have called
'After the Witch!' instead,
then somebody in the street might
have given chase.)

At any rate, Lizzy was left with
the book, so of course she opened
it, and saw on the first page:
'Friday Frightener,
to be performed on Friday the
Thirteenth only.'

'Why, that's tomorrow!' Lizzy thought, carefully spelling out the spell, which seemed not only perfectly simple but simply perfect for cooking Bella the Bully's goose in Chapter Two.

Chapter Two
In which a Spell is Brewed

Phew!
What a terrible spell smell!
Skinny Lizzy tried to clear the air
by wafting the kitchen door about
(still on its hinges, of course).

A good thing Lizzy had the house
to herself, or trouble would have
been brewing as well as that magic
mixture.

'Simmer for ten minutes, stirring
briskly,' said the spell.

Well, those were the longest ten
minutes of Lizzy's life,
but they came to an end in the
end, and there it was –
a deep blue ocean of potent
potion!

One mouthful of which, according
to the instructions, would give a
body navy blue stripes all over –
(hair, skin, nails, eyes, lips, the
lot!) –
lasting up to a week,
depending on the victim's last
meal.

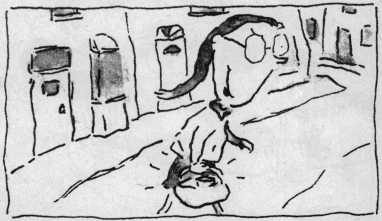

Giggling delightedly,
Lizzy emptied a can of Coke,
then re-filled the can with Friday
Frightener

and went off in search of Bella.

Bella was on the playing-field,
terrorising three little boys
by spinning them faster and faster
on the roundabout so they
couldn't get off. One was crying,
one was screaming, and one was
white as a ghost.

Lizzy held out her Coke can.
'That must be thirsty work, Bella.
Like a drink?'
Well, those who think Bella the
Bully will fall for a trick like that
have quite a surprise in store
in Chapter Three.

Chapter Three
In which a Dog is Kidnapped

With one great upward smash,
Bella the Bully knocked the Coke
tin flying out of Skinny Lizzy's
hands.

The dark blue liquid
spurted through the air and
poured a pretty wide puddle in
front of a pretty white poodle
which had just appeared, wearing
a pale pink bow.
The poodle licked daintily at the
dark blue booze –

and horrors!
In no time at all that dog sprouted
navy blue stripes all over, pale
pink bow and all!

Bella was so amazed that she
forgot to spin the roundabout, and
the three little boys escaped.

25

But Lizzy Lee leaped into action,
snatched up the dog, bundled it
under her jacket and fled before
its owner should appear.

'Don't worry!' Lizzy told the dog,
'I'll hide you for a week or so,
until you're back to normal.'
Lizzy knew that dog as Pansy,
spoiled pet of Mrs Martha
Mullins, Chairperson of the
School Governors, no less.

It was more than Lizzy's life was
worth to let Mrs Mullins find out
what had happened.
But Lizzy had reckoned without
Bad Bella.

When Mrs Mullins turned up on
the playing-field some seconds later,
calling: 'Pansy my pet, where are
you? Come to Mumsie!'

tell-tale Bella spilt the beans.

'That Lizzy Lee has maimed your
dog for life, and kidnapped it into
the bargain.'

Mrs Mullins made off like a
billowing Union Jack,
red with rage, white with worry
and blue with shock.
If she catches up with Lizzy,
murder could be done in Chapter
Four.

Chapter Four
In which Thirty Million
People Have the Shock of
their Lives

Lizzy was almost home,
intending to hide Pansy in their
garage which they didn't use
because they had no car,

when suddenly the poodle
leapt from Lizzy's jacket and ran
yelping down an alley into the
High Street.

There she made a bee-line –
(or should I say a poodle-doodle?)
towards soap-star Stella Simpering,
who was just about to scissor
through a ribbon to open the
hundred-thousandth
Asco supermarket.

So thirty million television news
viewers watched with awe as a
dark-blue-striped dog darted on to
their screens.

The incredible poodle pawed at
Stella; the cameras rolled;

'And so,' thought Skinny Lizzy,
'will my head in Chapter Five.'

Chapter Five
In which Rich Rewards are Reaped

Thirty million viewers' eyes
popped out of their heads.
A navy-blue-striped poodle?
Whatever next?
You had to hand it to the Asco
lot; they knew how to grab your
attention!

And indeed, the Asco lot were
delighted.
What rich publicity!
Better than they could ever have
dreamed of.
'Find that dog's owner!' cried the
Asco Chairman grandly.
'Whoever it is, I'll give him
free dog-food and free groceries
for life!'

It took the Publicity Manager half
an hour to track down
Mrs Martha Mullins,

40

by which time
Pansy had turned white again!
(She'd been off her food all day,
which meant the spell was
extremely weak.)

'Pansy, my poor little poppet!'
Mrs Mullins cried,
tenderly gathering up her pet.
'Did Diddums lose her Mumsie
then?'

But her sympathy was wasted;
Pansy had found her appetite
again and was soon tucking in
to the first free tin of dog-food
(as used by the world's top
breeders).

As for Bella the Bully,
her jealousy knew no bounds.

Pansy the dog was a heroine;

Skinny Lizzy was a heroine;

Mrs Martha Mullins was a
heroine.

Lizzy was reaping from Martha
not only all the credit for Pansy's
glory, but some of the free
groceries as well.

Grim-faced Bella made up her mind that in Chapter Six she, too, would share the loot.

Chapter Six
In which Bella Goes a Shade too Far

Bella ran back to the playing-field, found the abandoned Coke can and scooped up some of the spilt Friday Frightener.

If the dog could sprout navy blue
stripes for half an hour
with such splendid results,
then so could she!
And surely a navy-blue-striped
schoolgirl would make even
more of a sensation
than a mere blue-striped poodle?

If she hurried, the television
cameras would still be in place
to record her miraculous
transformation.
She would be famous!
She might even land a part in a
paint commercial.

Gulp!
The strange blue liquid trickled
over Bella's tonsils.
She pulled a face, for it was evil-
tasting stuff.

Then she looked at her hands.
Already they were turning stripy!

Delightedly, she watched the colour spread as she ran all the way back to the Asco supermarket.

Alas! The television crew had just departed.
There were two strikes, an embassy siege, a wage-snatch and a motorway pile-up still to cover, so no time to hang about.

What's more, the store was open
now, and offering free tins of salmon
to the first one thousand customers,
so the High Street was a heaving
mass of bodies and no one gave
Bella so much as a glance.

After hanging around
for half an hour
she trailed miserably home –
only to find that the blue stripes
had deepened,
not disappeared.

In fact, they showed no signs of
ever leaving her, no matter how
hard she scrubbed
– or prayed.

Bella's mother took one look at
her daughter, collapsed with
shock, and had to be put to bed
for a week.

Dad took to drink,

and Bella was left to look after
them both,
make all the meals

and do the chores,
while not daring to show her
stripy face outside the house.

It was easily the nastiest week of
Bella's life, and the most
significant.
For after it, when at last the blue
began to fade as slowly as curtains
hanging in the sun,
the miracle – the real witchcraft – was

that Bella's aggression faded
with it, and she hadn't the heart
to bully anyone ever again.